BRIGHT and EARLY BOOKS
for BEGINNING Beginners

D0407907

Marc Brown

WINGS on THINGS

A Bright and Early Book

From BEGINNER BOOKS
A Division of
Random House, Inc.,
New York

Wings!
Wings!
Wings!

They are wonderful flying things.

Wings flutter and flap
and they make things go.
Some go high and some go low.
Some fly fast and some fly slow.

Some wings are red,
some wings are blue.

Wings help you fly,
that's what they do!

Wings come in twos,

like twins and shoes.

Wings of many sizes.

Big
and small

and short and tall.

Wings on pets.

Wings in nets.

Wings are on eagles.
Never on beagles.

Always on ducks.

Never on trucks.

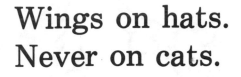

Wings on hats.
Never on cats.

Wings on chairs.
Never on bears.

Wings on dragons.

Never on wagons.

There are wings that drum.

There are wings that hum.

Buzzing wings that buzz
are dangerous to touch.
Those wingers with the stingers,
we don't like them very much.

Spooky wings
in the park

making sounds
in the dark.

Wings in a row

on a tree long ago.

Wings can take you
most any place.
There are wings
everywhere—
even in space!

Marc Brown

Ever since he was a boy, Marc Brown has wanted to fly, and once, at age ten, he tried to make his dream come true. Luckily his parents caught him perched on the attic window, open umbrella in hand, ready to jump. Since then he developed a fear of heights and a love of drawing birds, both real and whimsical. When he grew up, he gave up his idea of becoming a professional birdwatcher and became a truck-driver, a farmer, a short-order cook, a college professor, a tele-vision art director, and, in recent years, a well-known author and illustrator of children's books.

He lives in an eighteenth-century house in Hingham Har-bor, Massachusetts, where his two young sons keep him in touch with what children like to read. His oldest son, Tolon, was the inspiration for this book, Marc Brown's first Bright and Early book.